An American Spring

Sofia's Immigrant Diary

· Book Three ·

by Kathryn Lasky

Scholastic Inc. New York

The North End, Boston
1903

October 21, 1903

It is hard for me to believe that Maureen, my best friend in all the world, has been here exactly one week today. It seems as if we never were apart. Her bed is right next to mine and we talk all night long. Gabriella is always telling us to be quiet. But how can we be quiet? It is such a miracle — that she is here in the North End of Boston, that we are in this cozy room and not in that horrible hospital on Ellis Island in New York, where we first met and were quarantined. It is, as Papa would say, a *miracolo grande* — a huge miracle. And for me, talking in English with Maureen is the biggest miracle of all. When I came to this country

I did not speak one word of English. And Maureen, who came from Ireland, did not speak one word of Italian.

Of course there are the un-miracles: The greatest un-miracle is that Maureen is here because her mother died and her father had to go back to Ireland with the rest of the children. Father Finnegan arranged for Maureen to come here to Boston. The other un-miracle is my leg. Two months ago I suffered the illness called infantile paralysis. Dr. Balboni, our dearest friend, says it is a miracle that I lived and that my skinny other little leg that makes me limp is proof of that miracle. So that I live is, yes, a miracle but the leg is a part of me that died. So I think that is not such a miracle.

October 22, 1903

Maureen is in the same grade as me at the Paul Revere School. Miss Burnet, who was my teacher last year before I was promoted, is our teacher this year in fifth grade. She is the best and Maureen thinks so, too. I am so happy we get to be in the same grade. Maureen didn't have time for much school when she got to Brooklyn, where she lived until her mother died, but she speaks English so well that there was no problem with her being in the fifth grade. As a matter of fact Maureen is way ahead of me in arithmetic — she knows how to do long division. I am having a terrible time with that.

But it is hard to concentrate on long division or any schoolwork because we are all excited about this holiday that the Americans call Halloween. I think it is the same holiday that in Italy we called *vigilia d'Ognisanti*, the All Saints' Day. But it is celebrated very different here. You hardly go to church at all! You dress up in costumes, find scary places in the dark, and go around to people's houses to visit. Maureen said that in Ireland the holiday was mostly celebrated in church. So she and I are trying to think of costumes to wear. Gabriella said she would help us make them because she is such a good seamstress but that first we have to decide what we want. That is the hard part.

October 23, 1903

Good news! My good friend Chiarina told me that the Lilies of the Arno — the club for Italian girls that both she and I belong to, which meets at the North Bennet Street School on Saturday mornings — is planning a special costume making meeting this Saturday. And they will supply some of the material to make the costumes. Gabriella says she will go with us. So between today and tomorrow morning Maureen and I have to come up with some ideas for a costume. But this is hard. We have promised to help Mama and Papa. A new shipment of canned tomatoes came in from Italy and Friday, today, is always a very busy day with the weekend coming up. And we promised to come in right after the meeting of the Lilies and help some more tomorrow. I wish we didn't have to help. Our main job is watching my youngest brother Marco and seeing that he does not pull down the displays. He is into everything these days — and not even two yet! But as soon as he started walking he was, as Papa says, *big trouble on two pins*. I do not think that this is the proper translation from Italian, but it means that we have to chase him about a lot and I cannot really chase that much because of my leg. And that in itself is another problem. I have to figure out a costume not just for me but for my crutch, too. I do not need my crutch all the time. For instance not in this apartment because it is so small, or in the school classroom. But if Maureen and I go out and walk all through the neighborhood I will need my crutch.

October 25, 1903

So much to tell! There is good news and then there is, well, not really bad news but not so good news. First, the truly good news. Maureen and I thought of a terrific costume. It was inspired by working in the *salumeria*, Mama and Papa's store. Whoever would have thought that a delicatessen could inspire a costume? But it has. Maureen and I were both stacking the cans of tomatoes from Cento into pyramids in the window for display. The labels on the cans are so pretty. They show big juicy red tomatoes on a vine with the hills of Cento in the background.

"Tomatoes!" Maureen said softly. "I remember when we were in prison" — that is how we usually call our time on Ellis Island — "how you were always talking about food and the wonderful tomatoes. You made me taste them even then. Tomato girl! That is what I called you sometimes to my family."

I laughed and said, "Yes, and I should have called you potato girl." For that was all that Maureen ever ate in Ireland, she told me.

Then suddenly the idea burst upon me. "I am tomato girl! I shall go as a tomato for Halloween, a beautiful tomato from Italy."

I think everyone thought I was joking at first. Maureen blinked and said, "Well, I am certainly not going as potato girl."

We just began howling at that, it seemed so funny. And then I stopped. "No, of course not. We'll go as two tomatoes on the vine! And the vine can be my crutch!" Gabriella says that this costume is going to be easy because she knows where to get a bunch of cheap red flannel. So that is the good news.

Now the not so good news. Maureen has met the vile (a new word that I learned that I just love), the disgusting, the hateful Mrs. Thomasina Genovese, wife of Papa's first employer here in the North End. She is the snootiest (another new word I learned and love), most stuck-up woman ever. She is very rich and very proud and she came sailing into the meeting of the Lilies of the Arno like a full rigged ship before the wind plowing into

Boston harbor. She had her servant with her and also her stuck-up daughter Mirella. Mirella and the servant were carrying piles of fabric and trimmings for Halloween costumes.

"Ah! Miss Romano," Mrs. Genovese or Tomi, as I like to call her, said to the lady who helps run our club. "I have come to make a donation of fabric and items that these girls might find useful for their little projects." And then she went on and talked about money and how much she is saving us by being such a generous donor. Of course, her own daughter Mirella does not even belong to the club. Mirella looked down her nose at us the whole time her mother was speaking, as if to say this is a club for poor girls who cannot take private lessons like I do. Mirella takes piano and studies ballet. And then Thomasina Genovese looked directly at me and then Maureen. "Ah, Sofia is here . . . and a new girl."

So I say, "Yes, Signora." (It pains me to even be so polite as to call her Signora.) "This is my friend Maureen O'Malley. She lives with us now."

"Ah, yes, I heard about that." *That* she calls Maureen! Maureen, who is half orphaned, whose mother died and father had to return to Ireland — she calls her *THAT*! It infuriated me. But what she said next was worse. "Is it proper for this girl to be attending a meeting of the Lilies of the Arno?"

I can see that Miss Romano is completely confused. We all are, for that matter. Outside the door I see the shadow of a nun. It is probably Sister Lucia. She often comes to help out. And I see the shadow pause.

"What do you mean, Signora Genovese?" Miss Romano asks. "I do not understand."

I hear the rustle of the stiff fabric covering

Thomasina Genovese's big fat hips as she draws herself up tall. "Is this not a club for lovely little Italian girls, our dear little flowers, and not Irish ones who might profit more from . . . how should I put it, less . . ."

And then at that moment Sister Lucia came in. God bless Sister Lucia. I have never seen a nun look so fierce, and believe me I have in my day seen plenty of fierce nuns. But Sister Lucia says, "Now how would you put it, Signora? Are we not all God's children?" And then very quietly she says to Mrs. Genovese, "Would you please take your fabric. We have no need of it here."

Well, you could have heard a pin drop. Mrs. Genovese ordered her servant and Mirella to bundle up the trimmings and material she had brought and she sailed out of the room as if there were a gale force wind behind her.

October 27, 1903

Only four more days left until Halloween. Our tomato costumes look great. Gabriella is really a genius with a sewing needle. She helped Luca, too. But Luca's costume isn't that hard. He is going as a pirate, which seems to suit him perfectly! Not that he steals, but Luca — for a boy of only eight — seems to have a genius for finding gold, or I guess I should say making money. And he makes a lot of it down on the waterfront on Atlantic Avenue — shining shoes and delivering newspapers to ships on the wharves. He knows all the ships and the tugboats and the crews and sometimes even the captains. The three of us will go out together and I think Chiarina will join us and maybe my friend Mirka who lives on Salem Street.

We are going to draw a map for our Halloween visits. And since Maureen and I are the oldest and Luca the youngest we think we should get to decide where to venture in the dark. So first we make a list of the places not to miss, and we'll also visit places where we're certain to get nice treats.

October 28, 1903

We are having many arguments about the route we will take. Maureen and I think we should go to Copps Hill first and then over to the waterfront streets. But Luca says no, it will be too light out then and the ghosts don't come out until it is really dark. It's not that we're scared, it's because we want to pick up our friend Mirka and that is on the way to Copps Hill.

Later

We want Gabriella to go with us but she says she's too old. She's fourteen. That's only four years older than we are. But I must admit she likes to do boring things like sit around the Caffè del Sport with her friends and drink coffee with whipped milk, which I think tastes horrid. She has a lot of friends from her sewing class, but now she is so good at sewing that she helps the teacher and sometimes the teacher gets her extra work. Last week she had to go all the way over to Commonwealth Avenue with the teacher. A very fancy house with a fancy lady and three fancy little girls who had ordered fancy dresses. The dresses were trimmed in Belgian lace and she brought home some scraps of the scraps.

October 30, 1903

Today was Friday and the last day of school before Halloween. Miss Burnet made it so much fun. We had our usual spelling test but they were all Halloween words.

Then she read us this wonderful story called "The Legend of Sleepy Hollow." It's a story about a man named Ichabod Crane who had heard about the ghost of a headless horseman who haunted the countryside where he lived. One night Ichabod sees him as he is riding along. And the ghost chases him on horseback and throws something at him. Ichabod thinks it is the horseman's head but it turns out to be a pumpkin. It is a great ghost story.

Then Miss Burnet gave us little cups of cider and some cookies that she had made. Then we were supposed to have quiet reading time or writing time. So that is why I am writing this for my diary. I'll paste it in when I get home. I wish school could always be like this. I can't wait to tell the story at home.

Later

After school Maureen and I asked Mama for permission to go to Haymarket to buy a pumpkin. She gave us six cents, which would buy a good size pumpkin to carve. But when we got there we saw two cute little baby pumpkins and decided to buy them instead. What a bargain! The pumpkin lady only charged us four cents for the two pumpkins. So then we had two cents left over, more than enough for a foot-long piece of licorice — six inches apiece! Life is so much more fun for me since Maureen came. There is just something special about dividing a string of licorice exactly in half with your best friend, and buying two pumpkins so we can each carve one and they can sit side by side on our windowsill with candles burning in them.

Sometimes, though, I know Maureen feels sad. I heard her crying one night softly. She misses her mother. I would, too, and there is really nothing I can do about that. I told Mama about hearing her cry and Mama said all we can do is love her. Mama says that Maureen will grow stronger and happier as time goes by. But does that mean she will forget her mother? I don't think I could ever forget Mama or stop missing her if something bad happened. Oh, no, I cannot be having such thoughts. These thoughts are unimaginable.

Later

I cannot help having these thoughts. So I was wondering, if something terrible happened to Mama — if she died and then if she came back as a ghost — would I be scared of her ghost? That would be so sad. Sad for both of us — for me and for my ghost mama. Would she reach out with those cloudy white ghost arms through which the dark night swirls and try to hold me? And would her arms just pass through me like water as I ran away frightened (spelled it right, I see this time).

HALLOWEEN
October 31, 1903

Today is the day!! We are so excited. We have tried on the tomato costumes. They fit perfectly and we wrapped my crutch in green felt, then put streamers on it. So it does sort of look like a vine. Mama said we only had to help two hours in the morning in the shop. On our way home we saw Dr. Balboni and he said to be sure to come to his house, which is above his office on Prince Street, because he had many good treats. We stopped at the Caffè del Sport. Gabriella was there with her friends. Usually Gabriella never wants us to be around her friends. It's as if we are too babyish. But Molly, one of her best friends who comes from Ireland just like Maureen, invited us to sit down.

As a matter of fact there were a bunch of young people from Saint Stephen's Church, where all the Irish Catholics in the North End usually go — except for Maureen, who comes to Saint Leonard's with us. Molly offered to share her cannoli with us but we both said we were saving our appetite for all the sweets we were going to get when we visit our friends tonight. So then they asked us about going, to Copps Hill. None of them were going, of course. They acted as if they were much too grown up for such nonsense. But they started talking about the ghosts on Copps Hill. I really wished they would have stopped talking about it. It seems that there is more than just one ghost up there. Not just Paul Revere's. And just when they were talking about Paul Revere's ghost and another one of a slave, a beautiful girl walked up to the table. I nudged Maureen with my good foot. It was Rose Fitzgerald, the girl I had been telling her about. She's just thirteen but she looks much older and acts much older, too, but not in any snooty way. She has very black hair and pale skin and the most intense blue eyes. But the most amazing thing about her is her smile. She doesn't have one of those gushy, sweet little simpering smiles. No, when Rose Fitzgerald smiles it is as if her whole face cracks open in true joy. So there we were talking about ghosts on Copps Hill and she says, "Well, I heard that Cotton Mather's ghost is up there all the time — Halloween Eve or not."

"Who's Cotton Mather?" I asked.

Then just as prim as anything but with a devilish twinkle in her eye she says, "They say he was a preacher and a very scholarly man. Very smart. But seems he had a taste for hanging women!"

"WHAT?" Maureen and I nearly fell over dead. I guess we are the only ones who have not heard of the fiendish Cotton Mather, who more than two hundred years ago became convinced that the Devil himself was afoot in Massachusetts and was turning women into witches. Yes, witches! Not just the fairy tale *strega*, witch stories they tell in Italy, but real witches!

"Of course it was all nonsense," Rose Fitzgerald snorted. "But it was a bad time out in Salem for those poor women and two men and one child."

"A child?" I gasped.

"Yes, one little baby. Her mother, Sarah Good, had been arrested and gave birth and died along with the child in jail."

By this time Maureen and I had to hear the rest and so did Gabriella, for none of us had heard about these witch trials north of Boston in the town of Salem. Afterward all I could think to say to the lovely Rose was, "But why . . . why would they do this, why would he do it, especially if he was a man of great learning and a reverend?"

Rose just shook her head. "You can have all the learning but if you do not have faith, maybe it doesn't matter."

November 1, 1903

Resting up from Halloween. No time to write. But *mamma mia*, what a Halloween. We nearly got into big trouble.

November 4, 1903

All right. Finally the time to write all this down. Too bad it could not be my composition but I almost got into big enough trouble on Halloween anyway, so if I write about it this could send me to jail. Yes indeed the constable had one hand on Luca's ear, twisting it very hard, and the other hand on my wrist. And Maureen was about to attack — yes, attack — "an officer of the law," but luckily Dr. Balboni showed up just in time and that was only the beginning of Halloween. We had not even seen the ghost yet!

We set out just as dark was falling. Luca of course had his way, so first we went to the waterfront and visited the captain of the steamship *Sea Hound*. Luca knows the captain and runs all sorts of errands for him when he is in port — gets him his favorite tobacco, his newspapers, the schedule of the musical shows in Scollay Square. But Luca said Captain Grandby is a very nice man and had told him to bring us aboard. So we went and the captain gave us a tour of the ship. This was the first ship I had been on since coming to America on the steamship *Florida*. I have to say I don't miss ship life. This ship seemed even more cramped. But he gave us each some pieces of hard candy and had "Cookie" — that is what they call a cook on a sailing ship — give us a slice of gingerbread. So that was good and everyone liked our costumes. Although Maureen and I of course couldn't really sit down while we ate the gingerbread or we would have squashed our tomatoes.

Next we went to Gennaro Romagnoli's, the pigeon man. I had been meaning to take Maureen to meet him. You see, when Maureen was living in Brooklyn and so poor she could not afford a stamp to send me a letter we discovered that mail could be sent by carrier pigeon. Luca found this out and that is how we communicated. Maureen has been here more than two weeks and I still had never brought her to meet Mr. Romagnoli and Caesar, the lovely almost-white pigeon who flew back and forth from Mr. Romagnoli's rooftop to Brooklyn often as much as twice a week delivering our messages. If it hadn't been for Caesar I might never have seen Maureen again. Mr. Romagnoli was so happy to finally meet Maureen and he gave us chocolates wrapped in bright foil. We went up on the roof and met Caesar and Mr. Romagnoli also warned us never to give pigeons chocolate to eat, for it can kill them!

Then we were going to work our way back from the waterfront to Dr. Balboni's on Prince Street. We decided to cut through Fleet Street.

I had not even remembered until I was right in front of their building that the Genoveses, the vile, the disgusting, the hateful, the snobbiest of snoots Thomasina Genovese, lived right on the corner in their big fancy two-floor apartment.

I told Maureen that this was where that horrible woman lived. And she said, "Well, we're certainly not going to visit her."

And then, I am not sure how, you know these things just sometimes happen. There is no explaining them, but suddenly I said — it just popped out — "Don't be silly, we are going to trick them."

Luca's eyes lit up. "I got soap! We can soap their windows."

I'd brought soap, too, just because I had heard all the kids in school talking about it. I wasn't really sure what I would soap, but you know it seemed like this was an American custom. I'm trying to be American, so I brought soap.

"The windows are too high," Maureen said.

"But look at the door stoop," I said. Indeed the steps leading up to the house were made of very dark stone — soap would really show up well. Now I don't claim to be much of an artist but actually there are some things I can draw quite easily, like fat pigs with little curly tails. So I was drawing away and had just finished. Luca and Chiarina were admiring it. And then I began to write something like . . . well, actually I wrote in English, in my best cursive, *Mrs. Genovese is a fat snooty lady.*

Just as I finished Luca gasped. "Run!" But we were too late. A constable had just rounded the corner. This constable had the longest arms I have ever seen. He grabbed Luca by the ear and then in the next second had me by the arm. Maureen was just standing there frozen.

But all of a sudden I saw something blazing in her eyes, the fire in her face that flares as red as her hair. Her hands curl up and I am about to scream, "No! Don't do it, Maureen," when who comes round the other corner but Dr. Balboni. He stopped dead in his tracks. He looked stooped and tired and distracted. He blinked. "Sofia! Luca! *Che succede qui bambini?*" He was so stunned, he was speaking in Italian.

"Dr. Balboni," the constable said. "You know these hooligans?"

"Indeed I do know these hooligans. And what shenanigans have they been up to?"

To me it didn't even sound as if he was speaking English anymore — *hooligans? Shenanigans?*

"Making a public nuisance, defacing private property."

Dr. Balboni looked up at the building. "Ah, the Genovese family's house."

"Yes, Doctor."

"Let's see what has been done to deface this property." Dr. Balboni stepped up to the first doorstep. I was so worried that Mrs. Genovese would hear all this and come out. Then he peered down. "Defacing, you say. But I see a face drawn on this step." He looked up. "It is a very good representation of a pig. Who draws so well?" He looked directly at me. I felt my face get all hot even though it was a chilly night and the fog was rolling in on a cold breeze that smelled of seaweed and fish and autumn gales. "Pigs," he chuckled to himself.

I was dying the whole time Dr. Balboni babbled on. "I'll tell you what, Constable. Release these children to me, yes, and do unhand the boy's ear. I have already treated him twice this fall for ear infections. What a shame if the ear is now twisted off after the expense of all that medicine. Yes, children, in my bag here I have some nice carbolic soap and some sterilizing agents that will remove this. I think you can clean the steps up. Yes, yes. *Pronto, pronto!*"

And so the constable was dismissed and the four of us scrubbed away. The soap was so strong it did not take much scrubbing with the special sponges that Dr. Balboni had. And then we followed him back to his building on Prince Street where he gave us oranges and ropes — not just strings — of licorice and peppermint candy canes. Then he sent us on our way and told us not to get into any more trouble.

Well, we didn't exactly get into trouble. But there was to be even more excitement. Luca was now eager to go up to Copps Hill. I figured after what we had just been through and our narrow escape from the constable and jail, ghosts didn't seem that bad. So we walked over to Salem Street first and went to Mirka's house. Her mother gave us wonderful treats; the cookies she makes called rugalach. Then we set out. Mirka was very thankful that Halloween fell when it did — after the Sabbath had ended. The Cohens are Jewish and from sunset on Friday night until sunset on Saturday they cannot do many things. They cannot make a fire, or cook, or write, or even tear paper, or ride in a horse cart. Chiarina and I have a job where we light their oil lamps for them on Friday and make sure their stove has plenty of wood. They pay us ten cents each to do this every Friday. And they are going to find another Jewish family for Maureen to help out on the Sabbath as well. Mirka was dressed as some kind of fairy-angel-insect. I'm not sure what. But Gabriella had helped her, too, and she had some of the bits of that lace that Gabriella had left over from the sewing job. That should have been a clue right there for me. All right, I'll get to that later why that should have been a clue. Her wings were great, however. Her father had helped her make them out of cardboard and painted them gold, and they glued silver glitter on them.

So off we went. We went to the best houses on Salem Street and went straight to the top where the Old North Church is, where the lanterns were hung in the window of the steeple — "One if by land, two if by sea" — to signal how the British were coming at the start of the Revolutionary War. I had been up on this hill before and it always seems that it is foggy and it makes it all the creepier. Luca was leading the way and we cut over to Hull Street and then took a right onto Snowhill and went into the burial ground of Copps Hill.

Wisps of fog swirled through the graveyard, and some of the gravestones were so old and so thin that they reminded me of gaunt old men ready to be blown over in the slightest breeze. I was nervous.

"I want to find that old nasty fellow you told me about," Luca said.

"Which one?"

"The Cotton man who went about hanging witches."

We wandered through the graveyard and finally found the tombstone of Cotton Mather and someone named Increase Mather, whom Mirka said was his father, she thought. It was just feeling creepier and creepier to me. Pretty soon I was wondering whether I would rather be in the graveyard with these witch hunting fools and their ghosts or have been arrested by the constable for soaping the steps of the Genoveses. Then suddenly Mirka said, "Oh, wow!" We went over to where she was standing. The letters on the gravestone were dim and you could hardly read them. "Samuel Sewall," Mirka whispered.

"Who's he?" Luca asked.

"He was the judge at the witch trials. I read about him. He sentenced them to die."

"*Fantastico!*" Luca said.

"I don't think it's so *fantastico*. I want to get out of here," I said.

"You're scared!" Luca yelled. "Scared you're a witch and Mr. Cotton Drawers is going to get you!" Everybody laughed at that except me. I just started walking very fast, or as fast as I could with my crutch. Maureen and I had long ago given up being tied together on the "vine." I was heading straight through to the other end of the burial ground into the courtyard between it and the Old North Church, where there is a statue of Paul Revere riding his horse. Maureen was running now to catch up to me. She was laughing, I could tell. She wasn't nearly as scared as I had been. I was actually hot and sweating in my darned tomato outfit. "I'm going to get out of this tomato thing," I said as she came up.

I had just started to pull it off when Maureen suddenly gave a little yelp. "It's a ghost!" She grabbed me and we both fell down in a heap. I was half in and half out of my tomato. And I couldn't see anything. "What! What?" I kept yelling and then suddenly there was this big *ker-plop* on the paving stones next to us.

"It's a pumpkin!" Maureen screamed. "The headless horseman!"

What! I thought, and all this time I had been worried about Mr. Cotton!

Finally I got my head out of the tomato and looked up. Sitting right behind Paul Revere on the horse statue was a figure, a girl's figure with flowing white gauzy robes but no head!! She was sort of crooning and singing, "Whoooooo . . . whooooo, I am the white witch of the hill. I will never never be killed . . ." Now it was Maureen who was a quivering heap. But I stepped right out of my tomato. Yes, I stood there in my knickers and camisole.

"Gabriella Victoria Innocenza Monari, you get right down from that horse this minute!"

Yes, it was my sister. And then her friends Molly and Nina came out from the other side of the statue and said, "How'd you guess?"

Oh, so they were too old to go about in costume, but they weren't too old to play a trick or two.

I couldn't really be mad. I mean, it was a clever trick. But I figured that Gabriella owed me a favor or two after this. So my leg by this time was really hurting and I made her carry me piggyback all the way back to our apartment on the corner of Sun and Moon streets.

So this was my first American Halloween. And I shall never forget it.

November 7, 1903

We have started studying the pilgrims in school. I guess it is supposed to be interesting, but they seem to me to be very boring people. They wore lots of black, prayed a lot, and were very strict. Miss Burnet keeps talking about how brave they were, all the hardships they had coming across the sea in their tiny ship the *Mayflower*. But the Indians were pretty nice to them.

We have to write a composition and try to imagine what it was like to be a pilgrim.

November 8, 1903

Maureen and I were talking. We do not like this idea of writing a composition of what it was like to be a pilgrim. I mean, they were brave, but you know what? Maureen and I were brave, too, when we came here not even a year ago and were put in prison on Ellis Island.

We began making a list comparing our trip to the pilgrims'. Here's mine.

SHIPS and VOYAGE DETAILS

Mayflower	Steamship Florida
65 feet	200 feet
102 passengers	400 passengers
65 days at sea	27 days at sea
2,750 miles: Plymouth, England, to Cape Cod	3,201 miles: Genoa, Italy, to NY

Seasickness: a lot   I personally threw up
nine times

That is just the ship and voyage. So I'll admit that maybe getting here was harder for them. But once they were here at least the pilgrim children got to stay with their parents, while Maureen and I were put in quarantine all by ourselves.

November 9, 1903

Maureen and I have decided that we are going to change the pilgrim composition. Instead of calling it "What It Was Like to Be a Pilgrim" we are going to call our compositions "What It Is Like to Be a Pilgrim."

Later

I am a little bit worried about doing this composition. I really love Miss Burnet and I don't want to get marked down for not following the directions. But I do think that my composition will be more truthful if I do it my way instead of her way.

November 10, 1903

I'm still worried about the composition but I am just going to go ahead and do it. It's funny, but Maureen is not worried at all. I think Maureen is really braver than I am. Just like on Halloween, she really didn't get scared until the very end when Gabriella did the ghost trick. Maybe when you have seen your mother die there is nothing left to be scared of. I don't ask Maureen many questions about her mother dying. Sometimes she says something, but not often. One thing I do know is that Maureen was in the room when it happened. Her father had run out looking for a priest and the neighbors were taking care of the younger children. So Maureen had to stay in the room with her mother until she died. There is something so shocking about that. I just cannot imagine seeing your mother alive and then the next minute she is dead, even if she had been very sick. It is as if her mother crossed over this invisible divide.

November 12, 1903

Gabriella is getting a lot of sewing work. Through the sewing teacher at the North Bennet Street School she got a job helping a seamstress named Mrs. Wedge who has bad arthritis, especially in this cold weather. It is very hard for Mrs. Wedge to get over to Boston to do the fittings for the grand ladies who live on Beacon Hill and Commonwealth Avenue. So she sends Gabriella and now one of the women has asked Gabriella if she would be interested in making a gown for a friend of hers. She would not tell Gabriella the woman's name. She said that the woman guards her privacy, but assured Gabriella that she is a very elegant and fine lady. But Gabriella feels that this might not be fair to Mrs. Wedge. She is going to talk to Dr. Balboni about what to do. Dr. Balboni is always the person we go to for advice, medical or otherwise.

November 13, 1903

Dr. Balboni has come up with a good solution. He knows Mrs. Wedge because she is one of his patients. He says that what

Gabriella should do is be very honest with Mrs. Wedge, and say that she would like to take on this work, but that she realizes the lady who recommended her was originally Mrs. Wedge's client, even if the new customer is not. She should offer to pay Mrs. Wedge some money for the use of working on one of her sewing machines, since Gabriella does not own one herself. He thinks this would be fair.

November 14, 1903

Mrs. Wedge likes the idea. But this is the best part — Gabriella has asked Maureen and me to go with her to the lady's house to help carry the fabric to be shown to her.

November 15, 1903

A++. Yes, that is what both Maureen and I got on our pilgrim compositions. We are so excited. And Miss Burnet is posting them on the All School Bulletin Board. I have never had anything put up on the bulletin board.

Next week is a school Thanksgiving assembly and Mama says she will try to come. I shall show her the bulletin board then.

November 20, 1903

Oh mamma mia! Per l'amor del cielo! Dio mio! Yes, I can only exclaim in Italian. I have almost no words for the place I have been. The Fenway Court, that is where I have been! And the secret customer is Isabella Stewart Gardner, who I guess is one of the most famous and one of the richest ladies in Boston. I have

signs for what the specials of the
But I could see that as she started
r compositions her chin began to
d she clasped both of our hands and
em tight. Then out of the corner of
ught sight of Miss Burnet watching
ould see that her face had turned
d that her eyes looked all swimmy

er 24, 1903

out of school early tomorrow for
giving Day holiday on Thursday.
nvited Dr. Balboni for our first
ng dinner in America. I hope he
He has so many invitations because
the North End invites Dr. Balboni
giving dinner. But we are having
the day, so maybe he will be able

heard Papa talk about Florence and the famous Medici family with all their art and the Uffizi Gallery there. And I have heard people talk about the Vatican in Rome and the ceiling in the Sistine Chapel painted by the famous Michelangelo. Well, the Fenway Court is Mrs. Gardner's palace and I cannot believe it is one bit less splendid than anything in Florence or Rome. I know that it is called a palace because Dr. Balboni, when he heard about our visit, showed us an article in the *Boston Evening Transcript*. The article talked about a tea Mrs. Gardner had given "at her Palace," and how in the music room there were six musicians from the Boston Symphony Orchestra who played selections from Mozart.

I am glad that I knew none of this before we went or I would have been really nervous. As it was, Mrs. Gardner is scary enough. She has a face that is what Mama would call *tirato*, pinched and a bit pointy. She powders it very white and she wears very dark clothes that make her look even whiter. Her husband died five years ago, so I don't think that she is wearing the dark clothes for mourning still. I think she just likes black. We were permitted, after Gabriella had taken the measurements and we had folded up all the fabrics, to view the courtyard garden around which the palace is built. There is a high glass roof that covers the garden so that all year long, through every season, it blooms. Now imagine, here it is November in Boston and all the leaves have fallen from the trees and there is not a flower in sight. But in Mrs. Gardner's courtyard there are lilies, and immense roses the size of cabbages, and even palm trees, which I had never in my life seen. There were also orange and lemon trees!

But I guess Mrs. Gardner liked us, for we are

to come at least for a little while. Mama said that if he cannot come for the turkey maybe he can come for dessert. Mama says none of this pie stuff. She is making Italian desserts: lemon *panna cotta* and pine nut *biscotti* with dried figs.

November 26, 1903

Dr. Balboni came for dessert and guess what? He brought his lady friend! The one he once told us about who is a nurse at the Massachusetts General Hospital where he does operations. Her name is Lillian Dobie. She is so beautiful. She has red hair like Maureen's, only not as red. No one has hair as red as Maureen's. She wears her hair all piled up with tortoiseshell combs. It floats like clouds all around her head. But Miss Dobie, despite her red hair, is not Irish. She is from Halifax, Nova Scotia. Maureen and I got out our geography books and she showed us where Nova Scotia is. It's way up north and hangs out into the Atlantic Ocean. We asked her why she came here. And she laughed and said, "All there is up there is cod fishing and bad weather, except in summer. Summer lasts about two days." Then she turned serious and said that it was actually very hard for her to leave her family and that she missed them a lot. She is the oldest of eight children, but her only choice was to get married. There was no work for a young woman up there. So she borrowed money and came to Boston and took a nursing course.

Then the most embarrassing thing happened. Luca says, "Don't you want ever to get married?" I thought Maureen was going to pounce on him. I just screamed, "Luca! *Idiota!*" and then Mama started fuming in Italian. And by this time I was thinking, oh, my goodness,

Miss Dobie must think we're just a bunch of crazies. When our family argues or gets upset we are very noisy. But then Dr. Balboni interrupted and said in English, "Well, Lillian, before this family commits murder and mayhem. . . ." Of course we only understand the word *murder*, not *mayhem* — our English isn't that good yet. "I think we should make our announcement." Well we all shut up real quick. And Miss Dobie blushed very deeply as Dr. Balboni took her hand. "We plan to be married in the spring. A very small wedding, but you shall be invited."

We all burst into cheers and Mama of course was crying and went up to hug Miss Dobie who said, "You must all call me Lillian, please."

Later

I am so happy for Dr. Balboni. And I think that Lillian Dobie is one thousand times prettier than Isabella Stewart Gardner. I really think that I would rather look like Lillian Dobie and be a nurse than look like Mrs. Gardner and be a millionaire.

December 1, 1903

Maureen and I went to the meeting of the Lilies of the Arno club this past Saturday. Our project for this month is to make Christmas presents. Maureen wants very badly to make something that she can send to her family in Ireland. But she has so many brothers and sisters it will take her, as they say, *a month of Sundays* to make so many presents. It began snowing hard this Sunday and now on Tuesday it is really deep. The carts can hardly make it down the street. Our feet get so cold because we really do not have good boots. What do I mean boots! We have shoes. They come up just past our ankles but they leak like crazy through the button holes. Mama and Papa can only afford to buy us one pair of boots. We are five children, all different ages and sizes. So I do not know how we are to share one pair of boots. And I have very weird feet because my lame one is sort of twisted and shrunk up. Miss Burnet has brought to school dozens of extra warm thick stockings. As soon as we arrive in the classroom we are to take off our wet stockings and hang them on a clothesline to dry near the coal stove that she keeps burning in our classroom. Then we put on the warm dry ones that Miss Burnet has brought. At the end of the day we take those off and put our old stockings, which are now dry, back on. All day long, though, in school we are permitted to go around in stocking feet and that is fun.

If this snow keeps up I do not know how we will go to Mrs. Gardner's tomorrow as we are supposed to. And she is very anxious to have the dress finished in time for her holiday party season. She gives a big ball at the Fenway palace on New Year's Eve.

And I do not know how I will get to school tomorrow if it keeps snowing, because it is hard walking with a crutch through the snow.

Later

Mama and Papa decided that the smartest thing to do is to buy a pair of good sturdy boots in Gabriella's size since she has the biggest feet. Then we will take turns wearing them with extra socks so they will fit us. Marco doesn't need boots because he is so little. He doesn't go out in the snow that much and when he does Mama can carry him.

December 3, 1903

Guess who got carried to school yesterday? ME! The snow was simply too deep. So Papa carried me on his back and came to pick me up afterward. But guess what else? This is even more wonderful. When we got home, what pulled up in front of our apartment building but a big shining black sleigh with two fine, perfectly matched jet black trotters. There were two men all decked out in wine colored red coats with gold braid and top hats who were keeping the children off the sleigh.

When we came up one of the men said, "Miss Gabriella Monari, we are here for you and your sisters to take you to Fenway Court. Mrs. Gardner has sent us."

Well we all nearly dropped dead from surprise. And so did Papa. Gabriella ran up and got her sewing things and then the two men tucked us in under thick fur robes and off we went. How can I ever describe it, *é stata un' esperienza meravigliosa!* A most glorious and wonderful experience.

I had never ridden in a sleigh before. It was so quiet. There was only the whisking sound of the runners as we glided down North Street and out of the North End and then through Haymarket. And then we headed straight up Commonwealth Avenue. Dr. Balboni says that Commonwealth Avenue is the most beautiful street in the whole world — and he has seen a lot of the world. He calls it a *boulevard*, which I guess is a very fancy name for a street. In the center there is a wide walkway with trees on each side. And now these trees make a glistening white arcade under which ladies in fur capes and gents with top hats walk. The beautiful houses that line each side of the boulevard wear caps of snow on their chimney pots, and their wrought-iron fences and fancy grillwork have been embroidered with snowflakes. I feel as if I am in some sort of fairyland. Maureen and I hold hands tight under the fur blankets and no one says a word for the longest time. Finally I say to Maureen as the sleigh draws up in front of the palazzo, "I can't believe this."

Maureen looks at me and says the most curious thing. She says, "I can't believe the driver called us sisters." She paused. "Do you think Mrs. Gardner thinks we're sisters?"

So I say, "What difference does it make? I think we are." And Maureen's face crinkles up into the merriest smile I have seen her wear in a long time.

Later

Gabriella fitted the dress and it went very well. But this was the most interesting part. Mrs. Gardner introduced us to her friend the famous painter John Singer Sargent who was visiting. He had painted a portrait of Mrs. Gardner in the past, and when he saw the dress hanging up he said, "Oh, Isabella, we need to paint a new portrait of you in this dress!" Imagine if he does, won't that be almost as if he is painting a portrait of Gabriella as well? I mean it will be the dress that she sewed with her own hands. Although Mrs. Gardner designed it, Gabriella did make some suggestions that Mrs. Gardner really liked. I think Gabriella could become famous!

December 7, 1903

Oh, dear, Gabriella is not becoming famous — she is becoming sick! She started coughing two days ago, and now she is running a fever. But she is so worried about getting the dress done for Mrs. Gardner that she insists on working every spare minute. I happen to know for a fact that she cut school today and sneaked over to Mrs. Wedge's to sew. And Mama wanted her to stay home from school in the first place. But Gabriella realized she couldn't cut school to sew at Mrs. Wedge's if she didn't pretend to go to school. Mama would be so mad if she found out about all this!

December 8, 1903

After school, Gabriella asked Maureen and me to go with her to Mrs. Wedge's so she could show us how to turn a detail on the bodice and help her with the dress. We said we would go, but only if she would wear the boots even though it was not her turn. When she gets out in the cold air she coughs so hard it is scary! Between her coughing and my staggering along with my crutch in the snow it was slow going to Mrs. Wedge's, who lives over on Tileston Street. But Gabriella says that if we can finish turning the hems and the gored-something-or-other (I don't know all the fancy sewing words), the rest is just finish work that we can do at home by hand.

December 12, 1903

Gabriella is *really* sick. Dr. Balboni came to see her. He is very worried. She has pneumonia. He wants to move her to the hospital, but he is frightened that the move will be too much.

We had to miss a fitting with Mrs. Gardner. The sleigh came for us but we couldn't go. The two men who drive the sleigh didn't look happy. Dr. Balboni arrived just as Mama was explaining to them. You should have seen Dr. Balboni's face when they said, "Mrs. Gardner will not be pleased." I thought he would explode. He started to sputter in Italian and then he said, "*Momento!*" and asked for a piece of paper from my copybook. Then he scrawled a note to Mrs. Gardner. I don't know what he wrote but I have a feeling it wasn't so good.

December 13, 1903

We nearly lost Gabriella last night. Oh, to hear her breathing was a torture. Dr. Balboni slept in a chair by her bed. She seems a little better this morning. But it is now sleeting and rainy outdoors. Maureen and I have not been to school all week. We try to help Mama who refuses to go to the store to work. So either Maureen or I go to the store and the other stays here minding Marco, but even Marco seems to realize that things are bad and he must not be his usual loud and naughty self. Gabriella is delirious half the time and she is always muttering about the dress. I am so sick of this dress I could scream. But it seems to calm her if she thinks we are working on it. So Maureen and I sit there beside her bed doing the finish work. Oh, *Dio!* It is so boring. We must hand sew millions of seed pearls. The dress is supposed to be finished by December 20. That is just a week away.

Later

Well this is a surprise. Despite the rain and sleet we heard a commotion in the street below. I went to the window and saw the sleigh driver and his assistant. But I also saw Dr. Balboni. There is no sleigh but there is a large carriage followed by an ambulance. Then I saw two women. One is Mrs. Gardner and the other one is Lillian Dobie!

What is going on here?

December 18, 1903

I have not had time to write. Let me see . . . The last time I wrote, a carriage and an ambulance had pulled up at our corner of Moon and Sun streets. Well, Gabriella was taken to the hospital and put in a private room arranged by Mrs. Gardner.

Then once more poor Gabriella took a turn for the worse — almost as soon as she got to the hospital. Mama was hysterical, cursing Mrs. Gardner for moving Gabriella and saying it was the sleet and the rain that made her get worse. But I don't really think so because she was all covered up. Again Gabriella nearly died but Dr. Balboni rushed her into the operating room and performed an operation where he poked needles into her lungs and drained them. She began to get better almost at once. And of course the first thing she said when she came out of the anesthesia was, "How is the dress?" *Vestito? Vestito? Com'è il vestito?* Maureen, who doesn't even really speak Italian or understand Italian that much, just exploded in Italian. *Zitta sul vestito!* Shut up about the dress! It seems Maureen has mostly learned rude words in Italian.

So that was maybe two days ago. And right

now guess where Maureen and I are? At the palazzo! Yes, Mrs. Gardner still wants her dress. So seeing as our Christmas vacation from school started she asked Mama if we could come and stay at the Fenway Court to finish the dress. And now I must admit that even though sewing seed pearls is boring there are what Maureen calls "make ups," or things that make it worth the boringness. We have our own bedroom — there are so many rooms in the palazzo that Mrs. Gardner at first planned for us to stay in two separate connecting bedrooms, but we said that we preferred sharing a room. A maid brings us hot chocolate and buns and boiled eggs every morning, on a tray with beautifully embroidered linens. Then we go to Mrs. Gardner's *boudoir* where sewing tables and dress forms have been set up. All I can say is that it is lucky that it is only finish work that needs to be done. You have to work carefully but you don't have to do any cutting or fitting. Although Mrs. Gardner's personal maid is pretty good at helping us.

And it is not all work. We are allowed to go into the courtyard, which is all decorated for Christmas. There are twelve huge towering Christmas trees all with silver and white decorations and tinsel, and there are four hundred red flowering plants called poinsettias that I have never in my life seen before. It is so beautiful.

December 24, 1903

We finished the dress this morning. Four days late but Mrs. Gardner was happy nonetheless. It had snowed again and she sent us home in the sleigh. We must have seemed like Santa Claus arriving at the corner of Sun and Moon streets because she not only paid us the money for the dress but sent us home with a turkey, two hams, baskets of fruit, and four beautiful cashmere shawls. There was one for Mama, one for me, one for Maureen, and one for Gabriella. She also sent a special note to Gabriella and I have copied it down. Here is what it said:

My Dearest Gabriella,

Thanks to your sisters Maureen and Sofia the gown has been finished. But I shall always think of this as your gown. It was your idea after all to put in the four inverted gores that made a vain old lady's waist look youthful again — almost as slim as when Mr. Sargent painted me fifteen years ago. He shall paint me again in this dress and I shall refer to it as my first Gabriella Monari. You have talent and vision. You are more than a dressmaker —

you are an artist. Someday I am sure you will be as renowned as the great Parisian couturier Charles Frederick Worth, whose gowns I have worn for many years. When you are well, please come and visit me, for I have ideas for a new spring wardrobe. And I always give a summer ball to celebrate the rose season in the courtyard. Can you imagine a gown with a bodice fashioned from rose petals made of silk?

My fondest wishes to you and your family for a happy holiday.

Sincerely,

Isabella Stewart Gardner

Well, Gabriella could imagine those rose petals, for she sat right up in bed and asked that I bring her her sketch pad and colored pencils. She started drawing that night.

And there was more excitement to come.

Just before the rest of us were to go to midnight Mass, Dr. Balboni arrived with six pairs of boots! He said, "No one leaves this house without good boots! Not for Mass or anything."

We just blinked in amazement. The six pairs of boots gleamed in the light of our oil lamps. They must have cost Dr. Balboni a fortune.

January 2, 1904

It is the new year. Maureen and I ran out and bought a copy of the *Boston Evening Transcript*. Sure enough, there was a whole article about Mrs. Jack Gardner's New Year's ball in the society section. We couldn't believe when we read that Nellie Melba, the famous opera star, sang at the party! The ball was described as "a glittering affair" and then it went on to say that at the center "was Mrs.

Jack resplendent in a gown of deepest sapphire moiré silk that showed off a waist of which many half her age would be envious."

Maureen exploded at this. "They make it sound as if she really did have a slim waist. They should give Gabriella credit for the inverted gores. She would have looked tubby as a Christmas pig without those gores!" But Gabriella just laughed.

January 5, 1904

School started yesterday. We are beginning an exciting new project. I think I am going to like it better than studying about pilgrims. It is like a grand treasure hunt. Miss Burnet calls it the Freedom Treasure Hunt. You see, we are almost ready to study about the Revolutionary War. Boston is where it all began, and so much of it right here in the North End. But of course that is the easy part. You see, Miss Burnet is going to give us riddles. The answer to the riddle will be a clue to a place that was important during the Revolution. She gave us a special map that she made and we have to go to the place and mark it on the map each week and write a short essay about it. But that is not all. You have to notice something that was *not* there at the time of the Revolution. For example, a gaslight because they didn't have gaslights back then. This is going to be so much fun. We are to have it completed by Patriots' Day, which is April 19. And she promised that there will be a special surprise for us. I am so excited! And so is Maureen. We are going to start working on it right away. Miss Burnet says that all of the places are walking distance, except for the battlefield of Lexington and Concord, which is almost twenty miles away. So she doesn't expect us to go there.

The first clues of course are the easiest. Here is one:

This is the place up on Hill
On That Night there was a chill
One if by land and two if by sea
It was the glow of freedom for you and me!

You would have to be stupid to miss that one!

Maureen and I have figured out that everyone is going to rush out and mark their map and write their essay about all the North End places first because they are the easiest. But we're going to do the hardest ones first because we know that we'll be there all by ourselves and no one will copycat us.

January 15, 1904

This treasure hunt is *hard*! Now I am not so sure if we should have started with the ones outside the North End, because I am worried that maybe we haven't learned that part of the Revolutionary War history yet. So now Maureen and I are having to go to the library all the time to look things up. We have only solved one riddle in almost two weeks! And there are fifteen to go. We'll never make it by Patriots' Day at this speed!

Here's the one we have figured out:

*Two governors along with Peter and Paul
Four patriots who answered freedom's call
And now they share this shady place
Blessed are they in their grace.*

Paul we figured out — Paul Revere. But who was Peter and who were the governors?

We had to look up all the governors of the state of Massachusetts. It took forever. So the governors were Samuel Adams and John Hancock. But we were still stuck on Peter. It turned out to be Peter Faneuil. He was a wealthy gentleman who lived during the Colonial period and built Faneuil Hall. And the shady place they all share is the graveyard called the Granary Burying Ground on Tremont Street near the Park Street Church.

February 1, 1904

We have only solved one more clue. It was not quite as hard as the other one.

She was the first woman to set foot on land
But it is here she lies and no longer stands.

It was Mary Chilton, the first girl to step onto Plimoth Rock.

Maureen and I think that Miss Burnet has a great love of graveyards.

February 5, 1904

Today was the first day Gabriella felt strong enough to go to Mrs. Gardner's. We went, too, to discuss her spring wardrobe. It made Maureen and me feel so grown up when we were invited to *discuss*. I like that word. It is a very serious word for talking.

And Mrs. Gardner is very serious about her spring wardrobe.

She wants two suits that can go into summer, a tea gown, a summer ball gown, and (this is amazing) an outfit suitable to wear to a Boston Pilgrims baseball game.

February 14, 1904

Valentine's Day. I had never even heard of celebrating Valentine's Day the way they do here in America. In Italy and Ireland people go to special Valentine Day masses. Here everyone makes pretty cards and exchanges them. Maureen and I looked at my diary. We were in prison on Ellis Island just a year ago this day. It made us a little bit sad. There was one nurse, Nancy, the one we called Nice Nurse, and she made a little tea party for us and brought us paper and colored pencils to make cards. We made one for one old man who was also in quarantine. His name was Joe. He was a little bit like a baby with a simple mind, and Mean Nurse was so nasty to him. Well, we made him a card and he did love it, but a few days later he died. That is what makes us sad.

However now we hardly have time to make

valentines. There are just eight and a half weeks until Patriots' Day and we still have ten very hard clues to solve on the Freedom Treasure Hunt, not counting the easy ones in the North End. That means we have to do at least one a week.

February 17, 1904

Maureen and I are so mad. Chiarina and Mirka have been spying on us! They followed us and then saw where went for the clues. We caught them today just when we had solved the hardest riddle so far. Here is the riddle.

Old Sam was furious as could be
It was here he first said let's dump the tea.

All right, it was Samuel Adams and of course everyone thinks of the Boston Tea Party, Boston harbor. But you have to read the riddle carefully and then you have to read the history book. The riddle says where he *first* said let's dump the tea. And where he said it first was the Old South Meeting House on Washington Street. It was an easy place for Chiarina and Mirka to hide from us because it is at a busy intersection. They hid in the shadow of the awning of Raymond's, a variety store. But I spotted them.

We are so mad! I told them that if they didn't make it up to us I was going to Miss Burnet and tell. Then they would be in big trouble. This is cheating!

Later

Chiarina and Mirka came over to our house. We must have really scared them. So here is how they are willing to make it up to us. They will take one of the really hard riddles — we can pick it — and they will solve it and give us the answer. I was all ready to say yes. But Maureen — my goodness that girl is tough! "Not good enough," she said. She is so clever. She said, "Now Sofia and I are not going to ask you just how many times you have followed us." From the look in Mirka's and Chiarina's eyes I knew that it had been more than this one time. "But I think you need to go out and solve two riddles for us."

February 21, 1904

Well, they have solved one but still have one more to go, and we in the meantime have solved one as well. Theirs was hard. Here's the riddle:

The school has gone to the Fenway
But good old Ben decided to stay.

It's the statue of Benjamin Franklin in back of King's Chapel by the City Hall, and it marks the spot where the first public school was started in 1635. It was the Boston Latin School, and now it is in the Fenway near Mrs. Gardner's.

Ours was pretty hard, too:

Five men were killed in this clash
Including a black man who breathed his last.
Across the cobblestones blood did flow
Oh, it was a place of woe!

What confused me was the word *woe*. I thought that was a word to make a horse slow down but Maureen says no. She says it is an Irish word and means sorrow. The Irish have more words for sorrow than you can imagine!

Anyhow we figured out that it was the Boston Massacre. But what was hard was finding the exact spot. It was near the old state house that the men were fired on, or as Miss Burnet says, "cut down in cold blood" by the British soldiers. But there is no statue there or anything. You have to look really hard and then when you find the spot it is just a ring of cobblestones and there is so much traffic — carts, wagons, and coaches. We could have been massacred ourselves!

March 1, 1904

No more riddles solved.

March 5, 1904

Still no more riddles. And just over a month to go. We decided to start writing our essays on the easy ones in the North End.

March 7, 1904

I know that the pages of this diary must be thinking, if pages can think, that all I ever write about is the Freedom Treasure Hunt and clues and riddles. But something else really exciting happened today. Gabriella bought a sewing machine. Mrs. Gardner gave her some advance payment and with the money she had already made she was able to buy the machine. I know Mama and Papa really want her stay in school another year until she will be almost sixteen, but Maureen and I bet she won't. She is going to be able to make so much money working for Mrs. Gardner, and now other ladies are asking her, too. I think she will be tempted to stop school.

I wonder what it would take to make me stop school. I know I am not nearly as talented as Gabriella. So I think I'd better stay in school. Besides, I like it.

March 10, 1904

We solved one more riddle! Thank heavens, because I was really getting nervous. But we have "to keep at it," as Miss Burnet says. But I have been thinking a lot about what I would do if I didn't go to school. I said that I didn't think I have a talent like Gabriella's and I really don't. I mean I can sew — sew on seed pearls and turn hems — but she really, as Mrs. Gardner says, has vision. So I started thinking and wondering do I have vision? Oh, yes, I can see, but can I see in a special way? And then I thought, well I sort of can see in a special way. I am very good at finding these clues and solving these riddles. I could be a private detective. I could find missing people and solve crimes. But then I decided that I would have to stay in school for a while because it isn't like being a seamstress. I mean ladies will come to anyone who can sew well. But a kid just hanging up a sign that says *Private Detective*, like the one I saw on Washington Street when we were solving the clue of the Old South Meeting House — well I think if someone walked in and saw me behind a desk they wouldn't believe I could really solve a crime.

Later

I discussed this idea of mine with Maureen. She says that the problem is not that I am a kid but that I am a girl, and even if I were a woman no one would come to me. She says women can only be seamstresses, teachers, and nurses like Lillian Dobie. This really makes me angry. It makes me so mad that I think I'm going to just go out and prove it wrong. Maybe not now but when I get older. I said to Maureen that if I am all grown up and educated, and maybe even with a college education like Miss Burnet, and if I am good at finding a murderer, no one is going to care if I am a girl or a boy.

Maureen said, "Maybe."

Maybe isn't good enough.

March 12, 1904

Yesterday, I asked Miss Burnet if they taught private detection at Radcliffe College where she went to school. She looked a little confused, and she said she didn't think that they taught detection specifically but they taught a lot of things that might help me become a detective . . . like science.

March 15, 1904

I can't get this idea of being a private detective out of my head. I try and save my money to buy a newspaper whenever I can because I love reading about crimes. I asked Dr. Balboni if the police department ever hires women police officers. He said they usually only hire women as guards in women's prisons. Well I certainly don't want to do that. I want to catch the criminals, not guard them.

I should stop thinking so much about becoming a detective and figure out more clues on the Freedom Treasure Hunt.

March 17, 1904

We have solved one more riddle. But now Gabriella really needs our help with the sewing for Mrs. Gardner. The baseball outfit is turning out nice. But we have to stitch on these darned silk rose petals for that ballgown. The rose petals are not as tiny as the seed pearls but you have to be very careful when you stitch them on so that they don't crinkle up at the edges.

March 24, 1904

Maureen and I think that Chiarina and Mirka are getting ahead of us in the Freedom Treasure Hunt. This makes us very nervous. We have less than a month and still four more riddles to solve and we are behind in writing our essays and I think there are more rose petals on this dress than there are in Mrs. Gardner's courtyard. But Gabriella is paying us for this. We get a penny for every three rose petals. I don't know if I'm ever going to get rich this way. And also we are supposed to help out in the store.

March 28, 1904

Amazing! Unbelievable! Incredible! The vile, the disgusting, the hateful Thomasina Genovese has asked Gabriella to make a dress for her!! There was a picture of Mrs. Gardner in the newspaper in one of the spring suits that Gabriella had made and somehow Mrs. Genovese found out that Gabriella had made it. So now she is so impressed with us. She came calling and just tried to be so charming. She even gave Marco a tickle under his chin — she hates Marco! He ate that stupid doll's eyeball, remember! Anyhow, Gabriella was very gracious and told her that she would have no time for new *commissions* until fall. I had never heard that word before but it makes what Gabriella does sound so important. I love it.

April 1, 1904

Only nineteen days to go until Patriots' Day. I don't know if we'll ever make it.

April 6, 1904

All right, we are down to our last clue. But this is so tough. Here is the riddle:

On King Street near where blood was shed
Another rare gift was fed
With imagination that took wing
A true voice of freedom began to ring!

We've already done the Boston Massacre. So what could this be?

We are stuck.

April 9, 1904

Still stuck and only ten days to go.

April 11, 1904

Stuck
Stumped
Confounded
Bewildered
Nonplussed
Baffled
Mystified

Maureen and I are making a list of all the words that describe being stuck. We cannot figure out this riddle. We read it forty times a day.

The good news is no one else can, either.

April 12, 1904

Still no one else has figured it out.

April 13, 1904

We think someone has figured it out, but Miss Burnet has sworn that person to secrecy. We think it's Giuliana Forte. She is very smart. Miss Burnet says if no one has guessed it by April 15, she will give one hint each day.

April 15, 1904

First hint: The person was very against stamps but didn't dump tea.

Oh, thanks a lot Miss Burnet. What does that mean?

April 16, 1904

Second hint: We shall always remember the name Christopher.

Columbus? That was 1492. Please, Miss Burnet, I can't remember who Christopher is or was! And no one else in the class can, either. She says we weren't paying attention.

April 18, 1904

We figured it out. Phillis Wheatley, the black slave poet. She is the answer to the riddle and she lived on King Street with Susannah and John Wheatley. From a window in their house she witnessed the Boston Massacre, and the week before the massacre there was a shooting. A child died. His name was Christopher Snider. A Tory shot him and Phillis Wheatley wrote a poem calling him the first martyr of the Revolution. He was only eleven years old! Our age. How could we have forgotten Christopher Snider? His grave is in the King's Chapel burial ground, and Miss Burnet with her love for graveyards had already had a riddle that took us there to find his grave. We are dumb! So we went back to King Street today and we think that where the Wheatley house was there is now a bookstore. That seems right, doesn't it, seeing as Phillis Wheatley was a poet?

And now here is the big surprise. We knew that tomorrow is a holiday to celebrate the day that the first shots were fired in Lexington and Concord. "The shot that was heard round the world," as they say. But Miss Burnet has told us something very special. She says that really here in the North End we begin the celebration tonight at the Old North Church. She has secretly gone to all of our parents to ask if she may lead us to the Old North Church this evening, where the lantern was lit to signal that the British were coming. They are going to light it again tonight and we children of the Paul Revere School are not simply invited, but our fifth grade class will get to stand by as they light the lantern and carry it to the steeple window where it hung.

Maureen and I are so excited we can hardly stand it. It's so . . . so American!!

April 19, 1904

It was a fine spring evening. So different from last fall when we walked up to Copps Hill in the fog. Tonight the air was clear, the night was black, and the sky was embroidered with a million stars, but there was no moon, which made the stars all seem even more twinkly. We all walked together and my leg felt stronger than it ever had. I hardly had to lean on my crutch. When we got to the church the reverend welcomed us and he was holding the lantern right there. Giuliana Forte got to light it because she after all was the one who figured out the last riddle. But then we all got to go up to the window in the steeple where Robert Newman hung the lantern that signaled that the British were on the move to Concord to capture a cache of arms. And I had no trouble on the stairs with my crutch. We took turns standing at the window so we could see out and Miss Burnet read the poem by Henry Wadsworth Longfellow, "The Midnight Ride of Paul Revere." This is the poem that I recited almost six months ago when Maureen first arrived, when Mama and Father Finnegan walked into the school with my dearest friend in the world. What a surprise that was. And now here I was standing with my dearest friend and Miss Burnet's lovely voice is saying, "Listen my children and you shall hear/of the midnight ride of Paul Revere,/On the eighteenth of April, in Seventy-Five . . ."

I imagine him as he was so long ago, first being rowed across the Charles River with muffled oars from the North End to the Charlestown shore, where a horse was waiting. Maureen and I hold each other's hands so tightly. This is so hard to believe. A little more than a year ago I hardly spoke English and Maureen and I knew nothing of America except that horrible hospital where we were kept like prisoners for nearly a month. But now we have truly discovered America. We are pilgrims. We are immigrants. We are Americans!

Life in America
in 1903

Historical Note

Four years after the Pilgrims landed in Plymouth, Massachusetts, Puritans arrived in Boston. The Massachusetts Bay Colony, which was established in 1630, was headquartered there, marking the beginning of Boston's place at the head of Puritan life in the New World.

By the early 1700s, Boston had become the largest and most important city in New England. As a result, King George III of England placed heavy taxes on the people of Boston, and some of the people began to rebel. The movement to gain independence from England was born in the North End. The Boston Massacre and the Boston Tea Party further pushed the Patriots toward fighting, and the Battle of Bunker Hill — the first battle of the Revolutionary War — solidified their decision to become independent.

Boston suffered economically after the war ended, but soon recovered and entered a period of success that lasted until the mid-1800s. Shipbuilders, traders, and manufacturers made fortunes. Many of Boston's wealthy and prominent families supported the arts. Isabella Stewart Gardner made her home into a center for artists, such as the painters James McNeill Whistler and John Singer Sargent, both of whom painted her portrait. She built the lavish Fenway Court, to house her art

Portrait of Isabella Stewart Gardner by John Singer Sargent

collection, later opening it to the public in 1903. Today it is known as the Isabella Stewart Gardner Museum.

By the end of the 1800s, Boston's prominence was overshadowed by the westward expansion of America's borders, and New England's economic success fell as many of the once profitable factories closed. Thousands of Irish immigrants began to flood the city as the potato famine and starvation drove them from their homes. The city had begun to change.

The North End was the first home to many waves of Irish, Polish, Jewish, and finally, in the 1870s, Italian immigrants. The neighborhood began to be marked by poverty and disease as it suffered from overcrowding. But the neighborhood, comprised

Faneuil Hall

of one square mile of narrow cobblestone streets lined with Italian restaurants, crowded cafés, bustling markets, and delicatessens, was filled with the wonderful smells created by the Italians — wine, cheese, olive oil, and cannoli — that mingled with historical sites such as the Old North Church and Faneuil Hall.

A North End street

It seems fitting that the North End was the neighborhood where American freedom began, and that it grew up to be the neighborhood where so many newcomers to America continue to arrive, seeking that same freedom.

About the Author

Kathryn Lasky is the author of more than forty books for children and adults, including the first and second books of Sofia's Immigrant Diary, *Hope in My Heart* and *Home At Last*. She has also written four books for the Dear America series: *A Journey to the New World*, *Dreams in the Golden Country*, *Christmas After All*, and *A Time for Courage*. She is the author of the Newbery Honor book *Sugaring Time*.

Acknowledgments

Grateful acknowledgment is made for permission to reprint the following:

Cover Portrait by Glenn Harrington.

Page 102: Portrait of Isabella Stewart Gardner, by John Singer Sargent, 1888, Boston Public Library, Boston, Massachusetts.

Page 103: Faneuil Hall, Culver Pictures, New York.

Page 104: A North End street, Photograph #16919 by T. E. Marr — 1909 B. P. A. — File: Neighborhoods, Boston Photo: #96034 9/9/90, Boston Public Library, Boston, Massachusetts.

Other books in the My America series

Corey's Underground Railroad Diaries
by Sharon Dennis Wyeth

Elizabeth's Jamestown Colony Diaries
by Patricia Hermes

Hope's Revolutionary War Diaries
by Kristiana Gregory

Joshua's Oregon Trail Diaries
by Patricia Hermes

Meg's Prairie Diaries
by Kate McMullan

Sofia's Immigrant Diaries
by Kathryn Lasky

Virginia's Civil War Diaries
by Mary Pope Osborne

While the events described and some of the characters in this book may be based on actual historical events and real people, Sofia Monari is a fictional character, created by the author, and her diary is a work of fiction.

Copyright © 2004 by Kathryn Lasky

Library of Congress Cataloging-in-Publication Data
Lasky, Kathryn.
An American spring / by Kathryn Lasky.
p.   cm. — (My America) (Sofia's immigrant diary; bk. 3)
ISBN 0-439-37045-0; 0-439-37046-9 (pbk.)
[1. Diaries — Fiction.]
I. Title.   II. Series.
[Fic] 21   2003054460
CIP   AC

10 9 8 7 6 5 4 3 2 1   04 05 06 07 08

The display type was set in Edwardian Medium.
The text type was set in Goudy.
Photo research by Amla Sanghvi.
Book design by Elizabeth B. Parisi.

Printed in the U.S.A.   23
First edition, May 2004